KT-364-750

Contents

Brown-Ears at Sea

Brown-Ears is a floppy, lop-eared toy rabbit.
He is also rather forgetful. In fact, he is more
than just forgetful. He is positively careless –
especially when it comes to getting lost...
And so begins another adventure.

This delightful sequel to *Brown-Ears* will
bring a smile to anyone who, like McRoss,
has lost a favourite friend. It is recommended
for reading aloud to listeners from 4 years
and for reading alone from ages 7 or 8.

Stephen Lawhead is the author of nine books
for children as well as many best-selling fantasy
novels for adults. He lives with his family in
Oxford.

BROWN-EARS
AT SEA

More adventures
of a lost-and-found rabbit

STEPHEN LAWHEAD

Illustrated by
ROBERT GEARY

LION
Children's Books

Text copyright © 1990 Stephen Lawhead
Illustrations copyright © 1990 Robert Geary
This edition copyright © 2002 Lion Publishing

The author asserts the moral right to be
identified as the author of this work

Published by
Lion Publishing plc
Mayfield House, 256 Banbury Road,
Oxford 0X2 7DH, England
www.lion-publishing.co.uk
ISBN 0 7459 4777 8

First edition 1990
This edition 2002
10 9 8 7 6 5 4 3 2 1 0

A catalogue record for this book is available
from the British Library

Printed and bound in Great Britain
by Cox & Wyman, Reading

1

The Missing Sort

The trouble with floppy cloth rabbits is that they have little head for remembering things. Simple things: like where they are, or where they ought to be. They disappear. They go missing.

Now, you might think, "Oh, no! Not again! Another story about a silly toy getting lost!" And you would be right.

Truth is, things are always getting lost in this world. It seems to be a law of nature – like gravity, or sunrise, or sniffles in winter. Things just disappear, they vanish. And, I wonder, where do all the lost things go?

There must be mounds of missing socks alone. Did I say mounds? I mean hills, mountains of them gone astray. And what about umbrellas? And gloves? And buttons? Somewhere there must be forests of umbrellas, groves of gloves, and vast, shiny beaches of buttons.

Where this place is, no one knows. But Brown-Ears, because of his very bad habit of getting lost, stood a fairly good chance at finding out one day – if he wasn't careful. Which he hardly ever was, being a lop-eared, happy-go-lucky, friend-to-all, fuzzy cloth rabbit of the forgetful kind. Which was his problem to begin with: he was simply the missing sort.

Brown-Ears' current master, Ross McArthur McNelson McGregor McTavish Dundee – McRoss, for short – loved his friend Brown-Ears very much. Every bit as much as Brown-Ears' first master – who, by the most astounding coincidence, was also a little boy named Ross. (This first Ross had a brother named Drake, a very clever young lad, who, although he isn't directly involved in this story, wanted to be put in and I promised I would, so here he is!)

Both masters thought the world of Brown-Ears. And though Ross Number One had long ago said farewell to his lost toy, he still thought about him from time to time and wondered how he was getting on.

He needn't have worried. Brown-Ears' new master considered his floppy bunny to be such a special friend that he took very good care of him. He kept his fuzzy brown fur brushed, and his baggy blue bloomers clean and tidy. And he gave his bunny little presents: every time he found a

small length of ribbon, or a piece of coloured string he would tie it carefully round Brown-Ears' neck. His favourite thing was a bit of beaded chain – the sort with tiny brass beads that comes on rabbit's-foot keychains and such.

"This is for luck," McRoss would tell Brown-Ears as he fastened each new chain or ribbon around the bunny's neck. What the little boy meant, of course, was "This is for *love*." McRoss loved his floppy friend so much that he carried Brown-Ears with him everywhere he went.

Not that McRoss went to all that many places. Sad to say, McRoss had A Medical Condition – which meant that he felt tired and sickish, and had to stay indoors an awful lot of the time. He made frequent visits to the doctor and sometimes the hospital, for tests and treatments and therapy and such.

Brown-Ears always came with his master on these visits. Just having a friend along helped McRoss be brave. And McRoss would entertain Brown-Ears with stories, secrets, and the most amazing true facts. Facts like: the moon is really a ball of blue beeswax, and too much liquorice will turn your tummy black, and sticking out your tongue is good manners in Tibet.

Brown-Ears and McRoss were hardly ever out of one another's sight. That is, until that most awful day at the beach.

Did I say awful? I mean incredible, horrible, terrible, impossible – and any other 'ibles' you can think of! In short, a very bad day.

Well, actually it was a very *good day*. At least right up until the last dreadful moment when dear old Brown-Ears got lost. And that is where we begin.

2

A Day at the Beach

Picture this: a day in high summer, the sun shining bright in a clear blue sky, grass growing, birds singing, trees swaying in the balmy breeze . . . an excellent day for a trip to the beach.

McRoss had been taking his medicine like a good little soldier, and had begun feeling better. So the doctor told his mum that a day at the beach would be just the ticket. "A fine reward for a good report!" he declared. "It'll put the colour back into your cheeks, Laddie-buck!"

McRoss's mum agreed, and as soon as they got home she packed a big picnic hamper with cheese-and-tomato sandwiches (McRoss's favourite), salt-and-vinegar crisps (also a big favourite), green apples, Ribena (it's not a proper picnic without purple Ribena!), and four great big scones with gooey strawberry jam and cream. What a feast!

Into the hamper she also packed a cloth, a cross-word puzzle, two chocolate bars, and a thermos of tea. McRoss took his knapsack; he put in a game of snakes and ladders, a bucket and spade, a cricket bat and ball, a small paper kite, some string, and his most important toy of all – Brown-Ears, of course. They took a striped windbreak, and an old blanket, too. Then it was off to the bus-stop down the street where they waited for the big red-and-white double-decker to come along.

At ten past the hour the bus rolled up, they climbed on, and WHOOSH! away they went. McRoss liked to sit up top, right at the very front, so that he could look where they were going. The bus bounced through the streets of St Andrews, in the ancient and honourable kingdom of Fife, which, as it happens, has very nice beaches quite close to the centre of town. When the bus rolled to a stop a few minutes later, McRoss and his mum stepped out on to a grassy knoll, and before them stretched the sandy beach and the bright, blue sea beyond.

McRoss took off his shoes and socks and rolled up his trousers. He fished Brown-Ears out of his knapsack and they walked down the beach to look for shells while Mum spread the picnic. After lunch it was time for the kite, and then a game or two of snakes-and-ladders, and then a bit of cricket . . . and then a paddle in the shallow water.

"Are you having a good time, dear?" asked McRoss's mum when he came back for a bit of chocolate a little while later.

"Absolutely!" McRoss replied, and Brown-Ears quite agreed.

"That's nice," she said, "but I am afraid we shall have to think about going home in a little while."

"Oh, but I haven't finished my sand-castle yet," said McRoss.

"Well, you run along and finish it," Mum told him. "I think you just have time for that. But then we really must go."

"Come on, Brown-Ears!" cried McRoss. He snatched up the bucket and spade and the two of them hurried back down to the water's edge to where McRoss had begun making an enormous sand-castle. McRoss put the brown bunny on the top of the tallest tower and said, "You look out for pirates, I'll dig the moat."

McRoss dug a deep ditch all round the castle and set about filling it with sea water from his bucket. Every time he poured the water, it disappeared into the sand, which made McRoss cross. But Brown-Ears didn't mind not having a proper moat. The sun was so warm, the sea breeze so nice, he closed his eyes and settled back for a wee nap.

A little later, McRoss's mum called. "Come along, it's time to go!"

"Just a little longer," he answered. "Please, Mum? Oh, please?"

"No, the doctor says we mustn't overdo," she said. "But if you come now we'll get an ice-cream while we wait for the bus."

That was good enough for McRoss, so up he jumped, gathered his bucket and spade, stuffed everything into his knapsack and followed his mother to the Mr Whippy van waiting just across from the bus stop. They both got a 99-flake, and sat on the bench swinging their legs while they ate their treat.

After a bit, the bus arrived and they climbed on. McRoss sank into his seat, happy and exhausted. He put his head on his mum's shoulder and went to sleep. Ah, what a day! What a picnic!

And what a disappointment when they got home and discovered that bunny was nowhere to be found amongst all the bags and baggage. Brown-Ears was lost.

3

Of Time and Tides

Brown-Ears, of course, did not know he was lost. But that was not at all unusual. He was, as a rule, the very last to know. One moment he was closing his eyes for a happy holiday snooze in the sun, and the next he was waking up on a deserted beach in the dark. Well, not quite dark. But the sun was down and it would soon be night.

"Oh," said the rabbit, rubbing sand from his eyes and peering about. "I seem to have missed the bus. But not to worry," he told himself, "there's always another one. McRoss will come back for me."

How pleasant it would be to report that this is exactly what happened. But that would make for a very short story – not half as exciting as this one. Anyway, there he was, perched on top of the tallest tower of the sand-castle McRoss had built. It was getting dark. And . . . the tide was coming in.

Toy rabbits of a happy-go-lucky nature are not exactly wizards when it comes to things like ebbs and flows and oceany stuff like that. Brown-Ears had never even heard of such a thing as a high water-mark. (Have you?) And if you'd asked him what a tide table was, he'd probably have said that it was a table that had somehow got tied. Though why anyone should want to tie up a table, he really couldn't say.

Even if he didn't know about tide tables and such, Brown-Ears *did* recognize trouble when he saw it. And the sound of waves lapping nearer and ever nearer made it quite clear that he was in the thick of it. With every slap and splash the waves surged closer. Washing the far rocks, covering them, rolling on to the beach, covering that, filling in the footprints of all the people who had walked the sand that day, smoothing them away, rising, bubbling over the strand, closer and closer they came. Soon the waves were licking at the very edges of the castle wall. The toy rabbit could see the white froth sloshing into the castle moat as the moon rose slowly in the sky.

"Goodness," gasped Brown-Ears, "it is worse than I thought." He was stranded on a little island of sand which was his castle. The sea now covered the beach as far as he could see. "The moat and walls will keep the water out," declared Brown-Ears bravely. "They are very stout walls, after all."

Unfortunately, the moat and walls of a sand-castle are somewhat less stout than those of a real castle. In no time at all, water overflowed the moat and dissolved the walls into lumps of wet sand. Then it came gushing into the castle yard. When Brown-Ears looked again, the sea was swelling around the castle itself – washing big chunks of it away! And then the white froth was splashing right up against the tower where he sat.

"Not to worry," said our fuzzy friend boldly. "This tower is very tall – the water cannot possibly reach this high."

In saying this, the plucky rabbit showed how little he really did know about tides. As anyone in St Andrews could have told him, the tide was coming in and that meant only one thing: Brown-Ears was going out.

4

Instant Swimming Lessons

The inrushing tide can be a fairly startling sight to see – especially from the top of a crumbling tower of a sand-castle. Brown-Ears was certainly startled. More than that – he was staggered, astounded, flabbergasted. He was stunned, because he didn't know the tide could be so enthusiastic.

Sitting on top of his tower, Brown-Ears worriedly watched as the waves mounted higher. With each heave and ho of the waves, more of the tower washed away. Rather a lot, in fact. Not to put too fine a point on it, the tower was vanishing at a rather alarming rate. It put Brown-Ears in mind of a birthday cake on which he was the lone decoration left in place while the cake disappeared around him slice by slice. Or the solitary cherry upon a trifle being devoured by a horde of starving schoolboys armed with spoons.

"If this keeps up," observed Brown-Ears, "I'm

sure to get my feet wet. And," he added, "rather more besides."

It wasn't that he minded getting wet – well, not much anyway. He had endured getting lost in the wash and falling into the bath more times than he cared to think about; and once he had ended up in the toilet (don't ask). It wasn't the wetness of the water. It was that there was so *much* of it.

He looked at all the frothy liquid billowing around him and suddenly wished he had paid a bit more attention to McRoss's swimming lessons. He hadn't bothered at the time because cloth rabbits do not, as a rule, go in much for swimming. The bath was bad enough. But now, swimming lessons seemed a remarkably good idea; a solid, sensible idea.

"I wonder," thought Brown-Ears, "whether there is such a thing as *instant* swimming lessons? After all, there are instant potatoes, and pudding, and rice – all sorts of rapid foods, in fact. Why not instant swimming lessons?"

Certainly, he could use them now. Or a boat.

Boat! What a splendid word! What a wonderful invention! The bunny glanced hurriedly around. Alas, there were no boats in sight. No planks, boards or driftwood, either. In the gloom, there was very little of a floating *anything* to be seen. All he saw in fact was foaming sea water, and there was altogether too much of that.

"I *do* wish that bus would hurry," he remarked, trying to keep his mind off the rising water.

PLOOMP! CLOP! Another chunk of the tower collapsed into the sea.

"What can be keeping that boy?" Brown-Ears wondered aloud. "McRoss is usually so prompt."

What was keeping McRoss, of course, was the fact that he was already tucked up in bed, worn out from his day at the beach.

"Now, don't you fret, love," his mother had told him as he pulled on his pyjamas. "Your bunny will be all right. First thing in the morning we'll go back to the beach and find Brown-Ears just where you left him. It's too dark to search for him now, anyway."

Brown-Ears did not know this, of course. All he knew was that the water was rising higher, and the tower was getting narrower, by the second. If help didn't come very soon, there would be little point in it coming at all.

Just then he spied a very large wave curling towards him. "Hold on to your hat!" he cried. "This is it!"

The wave smacked the tower and splashed right over it, and right over the rabbit, too. Brown-Ears came up sputtering. "Salt!" This struck the brown bunny as extremely odd. "However did the sea get so salty?" he coughed.

A very good question, to be sure. And one

worth exploring in detail. Brown-Ears, however, had more pressing things to ponder just now. PLIPP! PLOPP! Another chunk of the tower disappeared.

"Help! Someone save me!" he shrieked. But there was no one around to hear him and help.

Another big wave came rolling along and ploughed over him. As before, Brown-Ears emerged spitting and sputtering. "I hope there aren't any more of those," he said with a shiver. "I don't know how many more I can survive."

If he had been paying attention – he wasn't because he was too frightened to do anything but shiver – he would have noticed that every seventh wave or thereabouts was a really big one. The next one, or the one after that, would surely carry him away. Brown-Ears didn't know that, because he had very little sea sense.

All he knew about the sea was what anyone could learn by lying on the beach: it was sandy and often crowded, and there were shells and seaweed and suntan lotion. He knew the sea was home to whelks and whales and the like, but that was nothing to do with him.

Until now. Oh, yes. Quite soon the sea would have very much to do with Brown-Ears!

5

What Comes In Must Go Out

The answer to Brown-Ears' question about how many big waves he might survive arrived abruptly. It was, "None." For as the very next big wave rose up and rolled towards him, the tower wobbled and started to slide. Before the wave even touched him, the bunny felt himself slipping with the shifting sand.

"Here we go!" he cried. PLOOSH! SLUNGE! The wave covered him, the tower collapsed, and away he went, tumbling along in the surf. At first he was merely rolled and pummelled by the water as it sloshed over the beach.

Now Brown-Ears fully expected to be carried off by the waves, and he was. Only he was not so much carried off as dashed back and forth, first one way and then the other, to and fro like a shuttlecock. One moment he would be heading out to sea . . . the next he would be heaving landward once more.

It made him dizzy. It made him seasick. Sliding first this way, then that, in a sort of giddy, roller-coaster up-and-down motion. Back and forth, forth and back. This went on for a long time – as if the sea, now that it had him, could not decide what to do with him. Take him, or leave him? Take him, or leave him?

Brown-Ears endured it as long as he could. He always tried to be a good sport, and whenever possible to look on the Bright Side. But in the end all the pitching and tossing got the better of him.

"Really!" he declared. "This is just silly. If I am to be carried off by the sea, I should like it to be a proper carrying off. Not this ping-pongy business."

He might have saved himself the trouble of complaining. The sea does what it pleases. Besides, if he had been observing carefully, he would have seen that he was in fact drifting out to sea. Slowly, it is true. But surely. With each wave that pushed him, another pulled him. And the pull was greater than the push, for the tide had reached its high-water mark. It had turned.

It took some time for the rabbit to realize this. But, when he finally did, he wished he hadn't been quite so hasty. "Now that I think of it," he reflected, "the to-ing and fro-ing was not so bad. I might have put up with a bit more of it."

But the tide was flowing out now – ebbing, as

they say – and poor old Brown-Ears was ebbing with it; floating on the waves, his bright blue bloomers ballooning around him like a baggy air mattress. With every rise and dip of the waves he saw that the shore moved a bit further away.

Soon he could see the bright lights of St Andrews shining in the distance. And those were getting further away, too. Brown-Ears peered into the gathering darkness and all he saw, as far as he could see, was water, water, and still more water.

"I had no idea that there was so much of it," he murmured. "It makes one feel quite small."

Small wasn't the word for it. Minuscule, microscopic, infinitesimal – those were better words. And Brown-Ears was gaining valuable first-hand knowledge of the meanings of those words. As well as words like jumbo, colossal, gigantic, mega-astronormous – which pretty well described how very immense the sea was turning out to be.

"I never dreamed the sea could be this big," he declared, watching the lights of St Andrews sink lower and lower on the horizon. "It is quite amazingly large."

Yes, it was. Nor was that all. The sea had more than a few tricks up its billowy sleeves – one of which happened along just at this moment: a great mass of stinky seaweed.

Brown-Ears discovered this as he discovered

most things – unexpectedly and quite by accident. A wave lifted him up and, when he came down, there it was. He was sitting square in the centre of the stuff. He took one whiff and wrinkled his nose. PHEWEE!

Phewee, yes. And stink-o pooh-eee, too! "A most unusual smell to be sure. I don't know that I've ever smelled anything so – so *lively*," Brown-Ears managed, tears coming to his eyes. Then, "At least," he ventured, trying to look on the Bright Side, "it is better than swimming."

Possibly he was right about that. And so, lying down on his smelly bed of seaweed, he drifted out to sea, and off to sleep.

6

A Rude Bird

All in all, Brown-Ears spent a most unpleasant night at sea: clammy, lonely, stinky, bounced here, there and everywhere by the waves. "If this were a hotel," he grumbled, watching the sun rise slowly in the east, "I would complain to the manager."

But there was no one to complain to. There was no one about at all. There was no one and nothing to be seen – but water. And the rabbit felt he had already seen all he cared to see of that.

So, with the next big wave, he rolled over on his back to have a look at the sky for a change. It was then he noticed that he was not quite as alone as he'd thought. There were sea-birds soaring high above him. "Gulls!"

Brown-Ears had never cared much for sea-gulls. He considered them pesky and pushy, unpleasant and proud. In a word: rude. No one likes a rude bird.

But, in his somewhat strained position – lying flat on his back on a mass of seaweed that was drifting slowly out to sea – Brown-Ears began to see the rude birds in a slightly better light. "Perhaps, gulls are not so bad after all," he thought to himself. "Perhaps they are merely misunderstood."

The more he thought about it, the more he came round to this point of view. "Yes," he declared at last. "I'm sure they are nice chaps, sea-gulls. Once you get to know them."

And he decided to get to know them at once.

"Yoo-hoo!" Brown-Ears called. "Yoo-hoo, sea-gulls! I say, yoo-hoo! Down here! Hello-o-o-o! Here I am!"

Whether any of the high-flying gulls could hear this curious greeting, or whether one of them merely glanced down and saw this pitiful wet rag of a cloth rabbit floating away and decided to investigate, I cannot say. However it was, one of them became curious enough to circle down for a closer look.

As the big, grey-and-white gull flew nearer, Brown-Ears waved and shouted his greeting. "Oh, Mr Sea-gull! Hello there! Hello!"

Gulls are naturally snoopy, so the bird swooped down and landed on the bed of seaweed next to Brown-Ears. He folded his long wings and watched the cloth rabbit with a bright yellow eye.

"Flotsam or jetsam?" asked the gull.

"I beg your pardon?" said Brown-Ears.

"Flotsam," repeated the gull in his grating voice, "or jetsam?"

"I'm afraid I don't follow," admitted the rabbit.

"Were you thrown overboard, or washed away?"

"Washed away, I suppose," the brown bunny told him.

"Flotsam," the gull sniffed. "Thought so."

Brown-Ears was impressed. "Really? How could you tell?"

The gull yawned, clacking his beak noisily. "There are only two kinds of people in this world," he explained, "them that are washed away, and them that are thrown overboard."

"Flotsam and jetsam," murmured the rabbit. "I shall remember that. My name is Brown-Ears, by the way. What's yours?"

"Sid," said the gull. "Got anything to eat?"

"Ahh," answered Brown-Ears thoughtfully, "no."

"Too bad." The gull stretched his wings and prepared to fly away. "See ya."

"Wait!" cried Brown-Ears. "Please don't go just yet. I thought we might chat a bit."

"Chat?" The gull folded his wings once more. "You want to chat with me?" He looked at Brown-Ears oddly. "Why?"

"Well," said the bunny slowly, "I've been floating out here all by myself for a very long time."

Sid clacked his beak loudly and fanned his tail. "Lonely, huh? I know what you mean. It does get lonely out here."

"Very," agreed Brown-Ears. "But at least you have other gulls to fly around with."

"Oh, that's all right – if you like sea-gulls."

"Don't you?"

The gull made a sneezing sound. "SNEE! SNEE!"

"Pardon?"

"*No* one likes sea-gulls," the bird said.

"Not even other sea-gulls?"

"Certainly not!" Sid puffed up his feathers importantly. "I may be a sea-gull, but I have my standards. Do you think I would hang around with a rude bunch like that if I had a choice?"

"I take your point. But I was just thinking – "

"It's *depressing*," griped the gull. "And I don't even like fish!"

"I'm very sorry to hear it," offered the rabbit. "But I wondered – "

"Tiddly fish, tiddly fish – every day the same," Sid continued. "Yuck! I *hate* 'em!"

"It must be dreadful," said Brown-Ears, and hurried on quickly. "But I was wondering if you could tell me where I might fetch up eventually?"

"Hard to say," remarked the gull, and pursued

his speech about small fish. "Have you any idea what they taste like? Why, after a day in the sun – "

"I'm sure I've never eaten a tiddly fish," confessed the bunny. "But," he pressed on quickly, "if I keep drifting as I am, where will I end up eventually?"

"Could be anywhere," Sid answered, and burped loudly. "E-U-R-R-P! Ack – tiddly fish. I hate tiddly fish."

"You were saying?" urged Brown-Ears, thinking that he'd really never met such a rude bird.

"Maybe Holland, or France, or Norway."

"I see," said Brown-Ears. "Well – "

"Or Belgium, Iceland, Greenland, Finland, Sweden. Or even Honduras."

"Really?" wondered the rabbit.

"Or then again it might be Spain."

"Ah, I . . ."

"Or Portugal."

"Oh, dear," replied Brown-Ears, who was beginning to feel slightly uneasy about all this geography.

"Or it could be the Canary Islands," continued the gull, who began preening his white feathers and looking for fleas. "Lots of flotsam ends up on the Canary Islands. And then there's the Azores, Gibraltar, or Venezuela."

"I had no idea," said Brown-Ears in a small,

worried voice. He could not imagine where any of those places might be.

"But I don't see that happening to you," said Sid, scratching his neck with his foot.

"No?" asked Brown-Ears hopefully. "What do you see happening to me?"

"I see you sinking."

"Sinking!" shrieked the soggy rabbit.

"Yeah – either that or getting swallowed by a whale." Sid, the rude sea-gull, stretched his wings again and began flapping them. "Are you sure you haven't got anything to eat?"

"Quite certain," Brown-Ears assured the bird. "But I would like to know more about this whale business. What do you mean by swallowed exactly?"

But the sea-gull wasn't listening. He was flapping his wings and getting ready to fly away. "Wait!" shouted the rabbit. "Where are you going?"

"I'm off!" called Sid. "If you're not going to feed me, I'm leaving this floating weed patch!"

And away he flew without a word of goodbye.

7

Alone Again, Naturally

"Dear me," thought Brown-Ears. "Dear, dear me. What next?" Getting swallowed by a whale had not even crossed his mind. And that was just the start! What if it weren't a whale? What if it were a shark? Or a giant squid? Or one of those sea lions one hears so much about?

Brown-Ears had never actually seen a sea lion, but judging from the jungle lions he knew about, the sea-going variety must be very big and ferocious indeed. With sharp claws and sharper teeth and . . . well, I'm sure you get the idea. A cuddly cloth bunny would not stand a fighting chance. Or even a running-away-and-hiding-under-a-very-large-rock chance!

All the same, maybe sea lions weren't the worst thing in the ocean at all. Maybe there were things lurking in the deep that made sea-going lions look like playful pussycats. Oh, no!

"That gull was a very upsetting bird," concluded Brown-Ears gloomily. "Still, it *is* awfully lonely out here, now that he's gone."

He raised his head and looked around. He did not see any whales leaping about, or ranks of shark fins racing towards him. In fact, all he saw was a clear blue sky coming down to a far distant horizon and bright water all around.

"This place is a desert," sighed the rabbit, feeling more lonely by the minute. "I wish McRoss was here."

Actually, what he meant was he wished *he* could be where McRoss was. Because McRoss must certainly be in a drier, friendlier place than where he was at the moment. Then again, it is often said that misery loves company. And Brown-Ears was one miserable rabbit.

Unhappily, he was soon to become even more miserable – if that were possible. For the further he drifted, the more water he soaked up. And the more water he soaked up, the heavier he became. Up to now, the seaweed had been holding him up. But then, just as thoughts of sharks and sea lions really got a grip on him, the seaweed shifted under his weight and Brown-Ears began to sink.

It was a very slow sinking. At first he didn't notice a thing. He closed his eyes for only a moment – or so it seemed – and was rudely roused from a tasty dream – something about gigantic bowls of lovely carrot ice-cream with hot alfalfa sauce and toasted sprouts on top – when sea-water dashed in his face.

"Yie!" he cried, waking up with a start. And then he noticed that he was resting much lower in the water than before, and added, "Eeeek!" for good measure.

Brown-Ears looked down and saw the little waves washing across his stomach. That was alarming enough, but then one leg slipped under the water. Whoa! He tried to haul it back, but succeeded only in sinking the other. Then his right arm sank. Followed by his body, neck, chin and left arm – in that order.

Being a rabbit, his ears were the last to go.

8

Going Down?

Gulp! Brown-Ears took a deep breath as the waves closed over his head. Down, down he went, falling slowly and tumbling like a leaf dropping from a tree.

Holding his breath was the right thing to do all right, but it didn't really solve Brown-Ears' problem; it just delayed things a little. What he really needed was a bus-ride home to McRoss. Besides, how long could he hold his breath?

How long can *you* hold your breath? Try it and see. Ready? Take a de-e-e-p breath. Now hold it . . . hold it . . . hold it . . . There! How long was that? Well, that's about as long as Brown-Ears could hold his breath, too. So now you know how he felt.

"What next?" wondered Brown-Ears as he sank lower and lower under the water. "I can't swim, and I can't hold my breath for ever. I'm sure to drown!"

Drowning is a danger, certainly. And Brown-Ears was so worried about drowning that he forgot one important fact: since toy animals do not actually breathe, they do not actually drown. They become waterlogged. Brown-Ears could hold his breath from now till a week from Thursday and it wouldn't make him any drier. And it was dry that he most needed to be.

By the time the floppy cloth rabbit remembered that he wouldn't drown, he was too amazed by what he saw to worry about the damp. Everywhere he looked he saw something fantastic. Why, the ocean wasn't a desert at all!

Most cloth animals, and more than a few people, do not realize this. From the top, the ocean might look like a desert – all flat and empty and . . . well, *deserted*. But, as Brown-Ears began to sink lower and lower, he began to see that the bottom of the ocean was not an endless stretch of sand and shells. He saw hills and rocks, mountains and valleys. And fish!

Where the air world has birds flying above the ground, the water world has fish. Lots and lots of fish.

Down and down he went. He fell right smack in the middle of a huge cloud of shiny fish: herrings, all bright and glittery, like so many silver spoons. "Gosh!" he gasped, "there must be millions of them!"

The herrings swam by him all going in the same direction. Then, all at once, they turned. Zip! Just like that. Quick as a blink. One flick of their tails and they were all darting off in a new direction.

"Excuse me – " began Brown-Ears, and ZIP! FLASH! They were gone.

Before Brown-Ears could wonder how all those fish could disappear so fast, he saw something else that made him wonder even more. It was a pale, blobby, frilly thingy that looked a little like a pillow made of jelly. And it was drifting towards him, quivering gently like a wobbly ghost.

"It must be one of those Jello-fish one hears about," Brown-Ears decided. "I shall ask him what is at the bottom of the ocean."

Brown-Ears waited until the blobby pillow was quite near and then spoke up. "Excuse me, Mr Jello-fish," he said politely. "I was wondering – "

But the jello – I mean, *jellyfish* paid him no attention at all. "I say," Brown-Ears said, raising his voice, "excuse me, please . . ." But it was no use. The jellyfish just flapped slowly by, trailing its long, frilly tendrils.

"Well!" sniffed the rabbit. "I've met friendlier puddings!"

Brown-Ears continued his long, slow sinking. Down and down, deeper and deeper he went. The water was wet, no denying that, but it was not as cold as he feared it might be. And once he had got over the worry of drowning, Brown-Ears found it almost pleasant.

"This is not so bad," he thought as he sank. "What's this? I think I can see the bottom." He looked around and saw that he was sinking down into what appeared to be – looked for all the world exactly like . . .

"I don't believe it!" Brown-Ears cried. "A vegetable garden!"

A garden, yes indeed. But instead of potatoes and tomatoes and marrows and beans, this garden grew sea cucumbers and sea lettuce and sea potatoes and other veggies of a nautical variety. And into the very centre of this enormous sea garden sank Brown-Ears, landing right in the middle of a great patch of sea lettuce, plopping down as lightly as you please.

If rabbits know anything, they know gardens. They *love* gardens. Because that's where they get carrots and lettuce and other rabbitarian delights. A rabbit's idea of the perfect world is one enormous vegetable garden from top to bottom. So, if you happen to be a cloth rabbit who is a specialist at getting lost, what better place to get lost *in* than a garden?

Think of it! Acres and acres of nothing but fresh green veg as far as the eye could see – all green and blue and shimmery, with dappled yellow sunlight streaming here and there over the lovely garden. Wonderful!

"And I have it all to myself!" he cried. "Wow! This is too good to be true!"

The trouble is . . . it was.

9

An Octopus's Garden

Brown-Ears had no sooner settled himself on a clump of lettuce leaves than he heard someone cough.

"Ahem!"

"Yes?" the bunny asked, and peering around he saw the oddest creature yet – part snail and part crab. The part that was snail was all coiled stripey shell, the part that was crab was staring at him with its long, waving eye-stalks. "Oh, hello," Brown-Ears said, "were you speaking to me?"

"Ahem!" the snail-thing said again. "Ahem!"

"Sorry?" said the rabbit. "I didn't quite catch that. Did you say something?"

"We haven't been introduced!" said the creature in a raspy whisper.

"Oh! Indeed! Please, allow me to make your acquaintance," the cloth bunny said in his most proper voice. "My name is Brown-Ears, and I am at your service."

"Pleased to meet you, Mr Brown-Ears. My name is Bernard," replied the snail-thing. "Forgive my asking, but what sort of creature are you precisely?"

"I am a rabbit replica. A cloth and cotton bunny, to be precise. In short, a toy," explained Brown-Ears. "I hope you won't think me forward, but what sort of creature are you, Bernard?"

"Not at all. I am a *Pagurus Bernhardus*."

"Excuse me?"

"Hermit crab, to you."

"A hermit, you say. How very interesting. I've never met a hermit before – crab or otherwise. How do you do, Bernard?"

"Very well, thank you," said the crab. "Most of the time, that is. Unfortunately, this isn't one of those times,"

"I know what you mean," sympathized the rabbit. "This is not one of my better days, either. What seems to be the trouble?"

"Good of you to ask, Mr Brown-Ears. But you don't want to worry about me. No, no. I expect you have more important things on your mind."

"I know I'm a stranger here, but if you tell me what's wrong, perhaps I can help in some way. After all, two heads are better than one, Bernard," Brown-Ears told him.

"My friends call me Buster," the crab said, and added wistfully, "but I don't have many friends."

"Well, suppose you tell me all about it, Buster."

"I'm sure you don't want to hear me moaning on about my troubles," said the hermit. "It's nothing to you."

"Go right ahead. I insist. And you never know — perhaps I can help."

The hermit crab seemed to cheer up at once. "Thank you very kindly. I shouldn't complain, really. It's just that I'm outgrowing my home. I must move to larger quarters soon, and I can't seem to find a bigger shell. I've looked everywhere."

"I'll help you look," offered Brown-Ears. "How would that be?"

This pleased the little crab no end. He began clicking his claws and thanking the rabbit, saying he'd never met anyone so helpful, thoughtful and kind.

"In fact," said Brown-Ears suddenly, "I have a pocket right here on the front of my blue bloomers. You could stay there until we found you a better place."

"Your pocket?" wondered the little crab. "Really? You'd let me stay in your pocket?"

"For a fact, I would — until you found a satisfactory shell."

The hermit crab wasted not a moment. With a

heave and a grunt Buster shrugged off the too-small shell. Then he quickly scampered on to Brown-Ears' lap and dived into the rabbit's roomy pocket.

"How's that?" asked Brown-Ears. "Better?"

"Absolute luxury! I can stretch out now. Ahhh!" Buster clicked his claws happily. "I can't thank you enough."

"It's the least I can do for a friend," said Brown-Ears pleasantly. "After all, you *are* letting me stay in your beautiful garden."

"Yes, it is a splendid garden. But it isn't mine. It belongs to Eldon. And let me tell you, he is very particular," said the crab. "A bit too particular, if you know what I mean."

Brown-Ears glanced around nervously. "I'm afraid I don't know what you mean at all. In fact, I've never been to sea before. This is my first visit."

The little crab pinched a bit of cloth in his claw, and said in a low, confidential voice, "Eldon doesn't like anyone messing about in his patch."

"Indeed!"

"In fact, it makes him quite cross."

"Cross, you say?"

"Ever so cross," said the crab. "He has quite a temper."

"Does he?"

"He throws things."

"Goodness!"

"And he changes colour."

"Remarkable!"

"And when he gets really angry he squirts ink all over the place."

"Oh my, no!"

"It's terribly rude, but that's Eldon for you."

"Well! I shall certainly try to stay out of his way while I am here," said the bunny. "Thank you for telling me."

"No thanks needed," replied the crab nicely. "I shouldn't mention it at all only – "

"Only what?"

"Only . . . Here he comes now!"

The hermit crab dived deep into the bunny's pocket, leaving Brown-Ears to face the octopus alone.

10

A Story a Day Keeps the Dogfish Away

An octopus not so much walks as he oozes. And, sure enough, Brown-Ears saw the octopus oozing over the rocks and through the lettuce, all eight legs – or were they arms? – curling and twisting as he came. Brown-Ears decided the best thing to do was simply to introduce himself and appeal to the octopus's good side. Whichever side that was.

"Hello, there, Mr Eldon Octopus," he called cheerily. "What a lovely garden you have here. I don't know when I've seen one better."

"What's this?" replied the octopus, oozing in for a closer look. He studied the bunny with his big googly eyes. "What have we here?"

"How do you do?" said the rabbit. "I am a – ah . . . a visitor."

"Trespasser!" corrected the octopus.

"Not by choice, I assure you," the lost bunny replied, and pressed on hopefully. "My name is

Brown-Ears. Ordinarily, I'm a dry-land sort of rabbit."

"A landlubber! I thought so. Well, Mr Landlubber Whosits," said the octopus. "Have you any idea what we do with trespassers around here?"

"I'm from Scotland, actually."

"We *eat* them!" The octopus glared at his visitor. "So, clear off – before I set the dogfish on you!"

Brown-Ears did not like the sound of that. "Oh, I should like very much like to 'clear off', as you so kindly suggest. And I would do so at once, if I could. But I can't."

"Why not?" asked the cross octopus suspiciously.

"I seem to be a bit lost, just at the moment – " Brown-Ears began. He noticed that Eldon was changing colour – from greenish-blue to bluish-orange. That wasn't a good sign.

"Right! I'm calling the dogfish!" The octopus raised a couple of arms – or were they legs? – in the air and began waving them about.

"Wait!" cried the rabbit. "If you'd let me stay for a day or two, I'd be willing to work for you."

The octopus stopped waving his legs and rubbed his squishy head thoughtfully. "What can you do, Landlubber Trespasser? Do you know anything about sea cucumbers? Or picking sea lettuce?"

"Not really," Brown-Ears admitted.

"Then it's the dogfish for you!" cried Eldon.

"But I can play games: Hide-and-Seek, Hopscotch, Statues – I'm ever so good at Statues. I could teach you some nice games," the bunny offered hopefully.

"Games! I hate games!" The octopus began thrashing his arms again. He changed from orange to shocking pink with bright red spots, and picked up some clam shells to throw. "Oh, dear!" muttered Brown-Ears desperately. "He's becoming angry. I'd better think of something else quick."

Just then he heard a small voice pipe up from deep in his pocket. It was Buster. "He likes stories."

Brown-Ears saw his chance and took it. "I have it!" he cried. "I know some very good stories."

Eldon dropped the shells. "Stories? Did you say stories?"

"Ripping yarns, tall tales, that sort of thing," Brown-Ears said breezily. "Fairy tales, fables, bedtime stories, amazing true adventures – I know them all."

The octopus turned from pink to a nice calm brown. "Are you sure?" he asked.

"Oh, yes," explained the rabbit. "My master has a story every night. I've heard hundreds and hundreds, and I have a very good memory –

except for where I'm supposed to be, that is. I don't know if you *like* stories at all, but – "

"I like stories," the octopus said, and made up his mind at once. "Very well, you can stay."

"You won't be sorry," Brown-Ears told him.

"Come on, then." Eldon the octopus gathered up the misplaced bunny in four or five arms and started for home.

11

Pinocchio is Not a Sneeze

Eldon lived in a rock cave near the centre of the garden. The cave was deep and dark, and a bit on the dank side, but it positively glittered with all the shells and shiny objects the octopus had collected. He liked bright things: wire, bottle tops, pieces of glass, bits of metal. He carried Brown-Ears into his den and put him on a rock shelf beside the entrance.

"What a nice cave you have," said the bunny, glancing round at the shiny knick-knacks. "It's so, ah – roomy!"

"Quit stalling," the octopus snapped. "Let's have a story."

"Right now?" gulped Brown-Ears.

"Right now, or I'll set the dogfish on you."

"Very well," said Brown-Ears. "Just give me a moment to think." Brown-Ears set himself to thinking. He thought for a while and said, "It's simply a matter of choosing the right one." He thought some more, and then said, "More a matter of finding the right story for the right occasion." He thought a little harder. "Really, it's all a matter of knowing one's audience," he said.

"I would have thought it was more a matter of knowing the story," remarked the octopus. "Are you *sure* you know any?"

"Of course I do!" replied the rabbit. "I'm just taking my time choosing one. It's no good telling the wrong story at the wrong time to the wrong audience. Where's the fun in that?"

"Just as I thought!" grumbled Eldon. "I'm calling the dogfish!"

"Wait!" said Buster. "What if you just told us the title and we could tell you if it fits. Would that help?"

"All right," replied the bunny. "*Pinocchio.*"

"Bless you!" said the crab.

"That was not a sneeze," Brown-Ears told him, "that was a title: *Pinocchio*. It's a story about a puppet that turns into a boy – or is it the other way round?"

"What's a puppet?" muttered the octopus.

"Why, it's a wooden toy with strings and you pull the strings and it jiggles and joggles and everyone laughs. Very amusing."

"Hmph!" The cross octopus picked up some

shells with two or three arms and flung them across the cave. He reached for more.

Brown-Ears wrinkled his nose and thought some more. "I know! *Winnie the Pooh!*"

"Pooh on you!" remarked the octopus, flinging another shell at the wall.

"No, no, you don't understand. Pooh – he's a bear. Not a real bear, you understand, but a toy. Like me – only slightly more famous."

"Bear?" wondered Buster, who had never heard of such a creature before. "Is it anything like a whale at all?"

"That's it! I've got it!" cried Brown-Ears. "*Jonah and the Whale!*"

"At last," mumbled Eldon. "Get on with it."

"This is the story of a man," the rabbit began, "a man named – "

"Ooo, we're not keen on *those* sorts of stories," the octopus interrupted.

"Excuse me? What sorts of stories?"

"The sorts with *men* in," explained Buster. "We don't like that kind at all."

"Perhaps if you would allow me to finish," suggested the rabbit delicately, "you might like this one."

Eldon the octopus grumbled and scrunched himself into a tight ball like a fist. He changed from speckled brown to bright orange.

"As I was about to say," put in Brown-Ears

quickly, "the whale swallows the man – all in one gulp, just like that."

The moody octopus faded from orange to brown again. "Why didn't you say so in the first place?"

"Now then, before I begin," the bunny said, "I must tell you the rules."

"Rules?" demanded the octopus. "Your story's got rules?"

"The story doesn't," Brown-Ears informed him, "but the storyteller does. Rule One: no talking during the story. Rule Two: no interrupting. Rule Three: no distractions. Rule Four: – now what was fourth?"

"No squirting ink?" suggested Buster helpfully.

"Oh, yes," said Brown-Ears, remembering. "Fourth: save all questions till the end. Got that?"

"I never heard of so much whoop-dee-doo over a story," grumbled the octopus, puffing himself up into something resembling a beach ball with a fringe of eels attached. "Phooey! I don't like it."

"I like it," Buster said. "Let's start the story."

"Ready?" Brown-Ears cleared his throat and prepared to begin.

Eldon may not have liked the whoop-dee-doo about the rules, but he did not want to miss the story. "Oh, all right," he muttered, wrapping five or six arms around himself. "Get on with it."

"Once, a long time ago, there was a great city

called Nineveh," Brown-Ears said in his very best story-telling voice. And the story was begun.

The octopus and crab made a fairly good audience. They only broke Rule One three times, and Rule Three twice. They broke Rule Two once, but only by accident, and they didn't break Rule Four at all. They enjoyed the story immensely. They liked it so much they made Brown-Ears tell it again the next night.

The night after that the plucky rabbit began *Twenty Thousand Leagues Under the Sea* – which took three nights because Eldon made him keep repeating the part about the Attack of the Giant Squid. When he finished that story, he told Eldon, "You've been very kind, letting me stay on like this. But I must be getting home again. My master will be missing me."

"But you can't go now," whined the octopus. "You just got here. Stay longer. Don't leave."

"I'm afraid I must. McRoss doesn't know what has happened to me; he's sure to be worried. I have to get back to him."

"I'll make a bargain with you," said Eldon slowly. "You tell me another story and, if I like it, I'll take you as far as the bay myself."

"Terrific!" said the rabbit. "I'll think up a good one." And he did. He told *Treasure Island*. It took five nights and Brown-Ears The Storyteller was never better – you should have heard him do Long

John Silver! But when the story was finally finished the octopus said he didn't like it, no, not one little bit: the rabbit would just have to try again.

Well, you can guess what happened. Every day Eldon would go out and tend the garden. Every night he would hear a story. And when the story was finished, the octopus would say he didn't *like* the story, and that the rabbit couldn't leave. The days passed. Brown-Ears began to wonder if he was ever going to get home again.

And he wasn't the only one.

12

Meanwhile,
Back at the Beach

The days went by, one by one, and summer slowly passed. Meanwhile, back in St Andrews, McRoss was sorely missing his good friend. On the days he felt well enough, he would go down to the beach and walk along the sand and gaze out to the far horizon hoping to see his floppy friend steaming into view on the back of a porpoise. Sometimes he'd just sit in the spot where he'd last seen his cuddly brown bunny, wishing, hoping, praying, that Brown-Ears would return. Some how. Some way. Some day soon.

I don't know if you have ever lost a very good friend. If you have, you know that it is one of the saddest things there is. The days are long and empty. The nights are lonely. It feels as if someone has hung an Out of Order sign on the world, and everything is dull and grey and gloomy.

McRoss's mother felt sad, too; not for herself,

but for her little boy. She gave him sandwiches to eat on the bus, and sat with him on the sand. She dried his tears when he cried, and comforted him as best she could. But she knew that when things get washed out to sea they never, hardly ever, come back. And she knew that with each passing day their chances of ever seeing Brown-Ears again dwindled a little more.

It was hard for her to watch her boy feeling so bad and she wished there was something she could do to make it better. All the same, she understood that the time was coming when they would have to face the fact that Brown-Ears was gone for good.

"McRoss," she said, as they walked home from another disappointing day of searching, "I'm afraid you'll have to give it up, love."

"I'll never give up," he said firmly. "Brown-Ears will come back."

"I know that you want him to," she said slowly, "but that doesn't mean he will. He might not be able to come back."

"He will come home. I know he will."

"Well, there is one last thing we might try, I suppose. And if that doesn't work – "

"What is it?" McRoss asked hopefully. "It will work. It just *has* to."

"When we get home, let's get out your crayons and make some posters," his mother suggested.

61

"You can draw a picture of Brown-Ears and say that he is missing. Tomorrow we'll take the posters round and put them up. If anyone has seen your rabbit they'll know where he belongs."

"Brilliant!" cried McRoss. "This is the best idea ever!"

That night they stayed up way past McRoss's bedtime making posters that looked like this:

The next day they put the posters up – three or four along the beach, a few in the town, one at the Tourist Information Office, and one at the quay where the fishing-boats came in.

When they finished, they stopped for a cup of tea and a biscuit. But McRoss could hardly sit still. "Hurry, Mum," he kept saying. "Let's get home. The phone might ring and we don't want to miss it."

Oh, his hopes were so high. His mum worried. Had she made a mistake in suggesting the posters? What if it only made things worse – gave him false hopes and great expectations? It would surely make his disappointment even harder in the end. Oh, dear. Oh, dear, dear, dear.

13

Something to Remember

It is so easy to worry, so easy to be afraid, so easy to lose hope. And once you've lost hope, you've lost something very precious. It's like losing your heart. Yes, it's really that bad.

But even when things seem to be at their very worst, we should not give up hope. We should never give up hope, because there is one thing that makes all the difference in cases like this. Do you know what it is?

Love.

That's right. Love always trusts, always hopes, always persists. Love never fails, and it never gives up.

While love may seem like a weak, small thing, there is really nothing bigger or stronger than love. It is made of very tough stuff. Nothing can shake it, or break it. Nothing can stop it.

Even when bad things happen, love is still

toiling away, sight unseen, smoothing out the rough edges, making up the shortfall, untangling the snarls, bending all ends to the good. Love is stubborn. It never lets go.

People will talk about how even the darkest clouds have silver linings, and how miracles will sometimes happen. But it is love they are really talking about. If dark clouds have silver linings, it's because love put them there. And miracles? Well, let's just say that there would be nothing of the sort, if not for love.

Love holds everything together.

That is worth remembering, I think. That is why I mention it just now – in case you, like McRoss's mum, had forgotten.

14

Falling Apart

Life in an octopus's garden is pleasant enough, if moist. But Brown-Ears was seriously worried about going home. Eldon, despite his promise, seemed determined to make him stay for ever. That was bad enough. But that wasn't all. Far worse was the fact that Brown-Ears was beginning to fall apart.

"It's my threads," the bunny told Buster. "I'm sewn together with cotton thread, you see. And lately I've noticed that I'm getting very floppy. More floppy than is good for me, I'm afraid."

"How's that?" The crab waved his eye-stalks helpfully.

"It's the salt water, I expect. It's rotting my threads. I won't last much longer. Just look at this." Brown-Ears held up one arm, which had become so loose that it dangled dangerously by a single weak thread.

"That's terrible!" gasped Buster. He hated to see his friend in such distress. "We've got to get you dried out at once."

Brown-Ears agreed, of course. The trouble was, Eldon secretly liked his stories – though he always said he didn't – and now that the octopus was used to them, he had no intention of giving them up. The rabbit was a prisoner.

"When Eldon comes back I'm going to tell him," said Buster. "He may not like it. He may get mad and throw things and squirt ink all over, but he has to be told. It's time we stood up to him."

Stand up to him they did. As soon as Eldon returned from tending the garden, Buster poked his head out of Brown-Ears' pocket and told the octopus about the dreadful thing that was happening to the rabbit.

"He's not made for the sea, Eldon," Buster said. "His threads are rotting. If you keep him here any longer, he will fall to pieces. We can't let that happen."

"Why not?" grumbled the octopus. "I didn't invite him here. It's not my fault."

"Oh, I'm not blaming you, Eldon," Brown-Ears said. "You were kind enough to take me in. Only now it's time for me to go. You must see that it's no good keeping me any longer."

The octopus dug several arms into the sand and began flinging it around. "But you just *have* to stay.

Please, I'm so lonely all the time. One more story. Just one more. Please? What do you say?"

"No," the rabbit told him firmly. "No more stories. I have to go. Will you help me?"

"No!" shouted the octopus angrily. "I won't help you. Why should I? No one ever helps me." He threw three or four sea shells against the wall of the cave. "No one cares what I want. No one cares about me."

"We care about you, Eldon. We both do. But Brown-Ears needs our help," said Buster. "And helping him is more important just now."

"I have to go home," the rabbit declared. "My master is waiting for me. If I don't go now, I may not make it home in one piece at all."

"Go then!" snapped the octopus. "Clear off – both of you! But you'd better both be gone before I get back . . . Or else!" Eldon puffed up and disappeared in a big black cloud of ink.

"I wish he hadn't taken on so," said Brown-Ears.

"Don't worry. He'll get over it," Buster replied. "Now then, we'd better get cracking. First, we've got to get you out of here."

The little crab climbed from Brown-Ears' pocket, gathered a bit of blue bloomer in his claws, and began tugging. "Whew! You're heavier than I thought."

"It's salt water," explained Brown-Ears. "I seem to have gained some weight since I arrived."

Inch by inch, the little crab hauled the waterlogged rabbit from the cave. Oh, but it took every ounce of his strength to do it. Soon Buster had to sit down and rest. "Don't worry about me," Brown-Ears reassured him, "you're doing fine."

"But we've only reached the entrance to the cave!" said Buster. "It'll take *years* to reach the bay at this rate. And Eldon could return at any moment."

"Too bad we can't call a taxi-cab," mused the bunny.

"That's it!" cried Buster. He snapped his claws with a sharp CLICK! CLACK! "That's what we'll do."

"Call a cab?"

"No, we'll call a cod," answered the little crab. "But we won't find one around here. Come on." Buster began tugging and lugging away once more, slowly dragging Brown-Ears from the octopus's garden.

They had a long, hard go of it, but when Buster stopped they were far away from Eldon's cave. "We can rest now," the crab said.

"Where are we?" asked Brown-Ears, peering around. The seaweed was thicker, and the water was darker and colder.

"This is where we catch the cod," explained Buster. "Sit tight, it won't be long now." The hermit crab crawled up to the top of a nearby hill and began waving his pincers in the air and whistling. In a little while a passing fish noticed him and swam over.

"You want a cod?"

"Yes, I have a friend who must get to shore. Can you take him?"

"To shore? No way. I don't go that far. Sorry." The cod started to swim away.

"Wait! It's an emergency," said Buster, " – a matter of life and death. He's got to get home. Won't you help us?"

The cod swished his tail impatiently. "Tell you what – I'll take him to the headland. He can get a skate to the bay from there."

"That'll do," said Buster. "I'll get my friend."

"Make it snappy, Jack! The meter's running!"

Buster scrambled back to the place where Brown-Ears waited, snatched the shoulder-strap of the bunny's blue bloomers and began tugging once more. "What's going on?" asked the rabbit.

"I have a cod waiting to take you to the headland. But we have to scoot; he won't wait long."

Pulling, jerking, tugging, towing, somehow the little crab managed to haul the rabbit up the rocky hill to the place where the cod waited. "Here we are! Here we are!" Buster called.

The cod took one look at the rabbit and said, "Hey! I can't take all that lot. Sorry, mate – you want heavy haulage." He swished his tail and was gone.

"Well! If that isn't just like a cod," muttered Buster.

"What are we going to do now?"

The crab clicked his claws impatiently. "Wait a tick! Why didn't I think of this before? Cuthbert is the fish for us!" Buster scuttled off. "Don't go away!"

"If I *could* go away, I wouldn't be here now!" Brown-Ears sighed. He looked at his poor, dangly arm. All the tugging and pulling had loosened it even more. His legs were looking none too good, either. And his floppy head was floppier than ever. He could see that it was only a matter of time before he began coming to pieces all over. "I do hope this Cuthbert is an agreeable fellow."

15

Cuddled by a Cuttlefish

Brown-Ears waited and waited, and just about the time he began to think that he'd seen the last of Buster, he heard a thin, squeaky whistle. Sure enough, here came the little pink crab – riding an odd, zebra-striped fish that flollopped as it swam.

"This is Cuthbert," said Buster, patting the curious fish. "He will take you as far as the headland."

"Very pleased to meet you, Cuthbert."

Cuthbert was not at all an agreeable fellow. Cuthbert was a cuttlefish, and I think that speaks for itself, don't you? He had two long arms and eight short ones, like a squid. But he could squirt ink and change colour like an octopus. This made him slightly confused, which made him crotchety.

"I'll bet," the cuttlefish sneered. "Want to go to Timbuktu? Cuthbert will take you. Cuthbert isn't doing anything important. But then, he never is, is he? Of course not. Cuttlefish never are. Pleased to meet you – Lah-Dee-Dah. Well? What are you waiting for – a royal invitation? Come on, come on, let's go if we're going. We haven't got all day!"

"Well, I wouldn't like to impose," said Brown-Ears doubtfully.

"Impose! That's rich. Ooo, wouldn't like to impose, he says! As if it mattered. For your information, Your Highest Highness, I was only sleeping. I get little enough rest anyway – I don't know why I bother."

"Really, I don't mean to trouble you," began the rabbit. "I didn't know you were sleeping."

"So that's all right, then," scoffed Cuthbert. "Buster, where did you find this creature?"

"Perhaps you should be going," put in the crab, before the cuttlefish could say something else nasty. "You two can get to know each other better on the way." He waved his claws at the rabbit. "Goodbye, Brown-Ears. I'll miss you."

"Aren't you coming, too?"

"Well . . ." Buster hesitated. "I suppose I could come as far as the bay. I've never been to the bay, but I hear it's nice."

"Great! Just great!" fumed the cuttlefish. "Let's take the whole sea-bed with us while we're at it! I'm sure there must be a few thousand starfish around who'd like to see the bay – and maybe half-a-jillion jellyfish. Oh, let's *all* go, shall we? Hmph! Give me a break!"

"We're ready, Cuthbert," the crab said, taking his place in Brown-Ears' pocket once again. "Let's go!"

The cuttlefish wrapped his two long arms tightly round Brown-Ears and, with a flutter of his side-flaps, they were off.

Contrary to what you might expect, being cuddled by a cuttlefish is not as pleasant as it sounds. It is, in fact, rather the opposite, if you know what I mean. But Brown-Ears, the Always Looking On The Bright Side Bunny, did not complain. He tried his best to enjoy the trip.

Cuthbert swam for a long time. Past rock gardens and under-water beaches, and seaweed forests of red and green and purple, over hills and valleys, canyons and chasms, gorges, gulches and gullies. They saw fish of all kinds: masses of mackerel, hosts of haddock, and mobs of mullet. They saw starfish and scallops by the score, and so many other things that Brown-Ears could hardly believe his eyes.

At last they came to a very rocky place that looked like the foothills of a mountain range, and the cuttlefish began to slow down. "We're almost there," said Buster, peeking out of Brown-Ears' pocket. "At least, I think we must be getting close."

"Close!" cried Cuthbert. "Well, thank you very much for that! I'm well past the point of physical exhaustion carrying this load, and all Mr Clicky Claws can say is that he rather thinks we might be getting jolly close, and, What Ho! Anyone for a cucumber sandwich?"

"Don't be so difficult, Cuthbert," soothed the crab. "All I meant was that, seeing as we've been swimming all this time, we must be getting close to our destination. Besides, we don't even have any cucumber sandwiches."

"*Difficult? Me?*" snarled Cuthbert. "Right! That's it! I'm finished! And oh, look! What a coincidence – here we are!"

"Here?" Brown-Ears wondered. "It doesn't look like anywhere that I remember."

"It doesn't look like anywhere at all," Buster added.

"Picky, picky, picky," mocked the cuttlefish. "You don't like the looks of the place. Is this *my* fault? Is this *my* problem? And to think I could have migrated to Jamaica. But no-o-o!"

Buster looked around doubtfully. "Where is the bay, exactly?"

Cuthbert released Brown-Ears and backed away. "The bay is that way," he said, waving a long, loopy arm in a vaguely westerly direction. "If you want it exactly, get a map!"

"But – " began Buster.

"Would you believe it?" muttered Cuthbert. "I don't know, you do your best for some people and what do you get? Not a word of thanks for your trouble. But then, I don't suppose cuttle-fish deserve any better. Still, one hopes. Silly, I know . . ."

"Hey! You can't leave us here like this!" shouted Buster, clicking his claws and whistling.

"Can, and did," replied the cuttlefish, speeding away. "I'm off."

16

What Goes Out Must Come In

Cuthbert flollopped away, leaving the two friends sitting on a big boulder at the bottom of a huge mountain of tumbled rocks. The sunlight shimmered on the surface far, far above, sending shafts of sunbeams sparkling all around them.

"It's very pretty here," Brown-Ears pointed out. "It's nice and bright. Just the place for a little sit down."

"The bay is that way," said Buster, trying to sound confident. "Now to find a skate to take us to the shore."

"I think I should warn you," Brown-Ears confessed, "I really don't know the first thing about roller skating."

"A skate, a skate – it's a kind of fish," explained Buster. "Very flat – like a flounder, only fancier. Nice chaps, skates." The hermit crab climbed from the rabbit's pocket and started off over the rocks.

"Now, you wait here and I'll be back before you know it."

Too true. Buster had not travelled more than a few inches when a big, blue, curving claw flashed up out of a crack in a rock and snapped shut right in front of his face. CLIPP! SNASH!

ZIP! The crab scurried back into Brown-Ears' pocket.

Brown-Ears sat up with a start. "What was that?"

"Lobster!" Buster screeched. "Whew! That was close. But there are probably lots more around. They live in the rocks."

"Are they dangerous?"

"Well, let me put it as delicately as possible: we're seafood."

"What do you mean?"

"I mean," explained Buster, "lobsters are the worst. They're low-down, mean and nasty. They're cross and crusty and cruel, and not at all nice. They eat with their fingers, and hardly ever clean their rooms or take a bath. What is more, they think the ocean is one big buffet – why, they'll eat anything that moves. We can't twitch an inch, or we're lobster lunch."

"We'll see about that!" declared Brown-Ears. "I haven't come this far to end up the main course at a lobster feast."

How to avoid it – that was the tricky bit. And

that would take some thought. The bunny and crab were sitting on their rock, trying very calmly, very quietly, to find a way out of their predicament, when up from the crevice in front of them appeared a great, ugly, tooth-filled mouth. YIKES!

Double YIKES! And YUCK! for good measure.

"Help! Look out!" the crab cried, ducking into Brown-Ears' pocket. "It's an eel!"

The cloth rabbit had never seen an eel close up before, but now that he did, he knew he didn't like them. Most people feel the same way. Just to *see* an eel explains an awful lot; most people do not require more of an introduction than that.

And wouldn't you know it? Everything lobsters are, eels are – only more. Grouchy? Low-down? Mean? Eels are twice as grouchy, low-down and mean as any old lobster. Nasty? Why, eels make lobsters look absolutely jolly. If anyone gave out prizes for nastiness, eels would win every time. No contest.

The eel squirmed and waved, snapping its toothy jaws and grimacing. Happily – if you can call this "happy" – the awful thing did not come out of its hole. But it didn't go away, either. It stayed just where it was – all slimy and snaky, glowering with its evil eyes. Every now and then it would SWOOP! at them, snap its jaws, and gnash its teeth. SWOOP! SNAP! GNASH!

Brown-Ears looked at the long, snaky creature, with its pinched-up face, glowering eyes, and mouth full of jagged teeth, and knew he'd seldom seen a more discouraging sight.

"We're seafood!" wailed Buster.

"We do seem to be in a jam," agreed Brown-Ears.

They were in a jam, all right, and a pickle, too. Did I say pickle? I mean danger deep and dire, doom and gloom, calamity and ruin. In short, between a rock and a hard spot. They couldn't move or hungry lobsters would grab them, and they couldn't stay where they were or a hungry eel would grab them. Either way: seafood.

"That means there's only one thing to do," said Brown-Ears bravely.

"Hide?"

"Nonsense," replied the bunny, "we'll just go another way."

"Eels on one side, lobsters on the other," cried the crab miserably, "just which way do you propose to go?"

The plucky rabbit gazed round thoughtfully, and at last happened to glance up at the sunlight glimmering on the surface far above them. "Up!" he said confidently. "We go up."

"Hiding is better. You have almost half a chance if you hide."

"What goes out must come in," Brown-Ears told the crab.

"I'm not sure I follow," said Buster.

"I went out with the tide," explained the bunny. "Maybe the tide will bring me in again. Anyway, it's better than staying here." At last the rabbit was showing some sea sense. "Now then, if we just climb up these rocks to the surface, I think the tide will take us the rest of the way."

The little crab gazed up at all the long way they had to climb. "I don't know," he said, "it's awfully far."

"Don't worry about that. We'll just take it one step at a time," Brown-Ears said. "You climb, and I'll keep a sharp look-out for eels."

17

The Long, Hard Climb

Buster gripped one strap of the cloth bunny's blue bloomers in one of his strong claws, and hooked a rock with the other. With a grunt and a groan he began climbing. One step at a time, dragging the waterlogged rabbit behind him. BUMP-A-LUMP! BUMP-A-LUMP! Up, up, and over the rocks.

Brown-Ears endured the bumps and scrapes and snags, and watched for hungry eels. Buster held tight to his friend, slowly, slowly, pulling them both up. Brown-Ears kept getting caught up; his bloomers snagged, his arms and legs were wrenched this way and that. Oh, it was hard, hard work. But they kept on.

After a while, they noticed that the water seemed a little warmer. And then they saw that it was getting lighter, too. And that there were small fish darting here and there among rocks, and the rocks had barnacles and limpets and tiny crusty thingies on them. Finally, after a very long time indeed – and more bumps, lumps, and snags than Brown-Ears could bear to think about – Buster announced, "I can hear the waves! We're almost there!"

"Well done!" cried Brown-Ears. "I knew you could do it. Buster, you're a hero!"

And he might have gone on congratulating the little crab, but before they could even breathe a sigh of relief a swift-gliding shadow passed over them.

"Shark!" cried Buster, diving back into Brown-Ears' pocket in a flash.

"Shark?" the rabbit said, turning his eyes towards the shimmering surface. "Where?"

"Oh, lobsters and eels weren't bad enough. Now we have to have sharks!"

Another smooth shadow passed over them, and Brown-Ears saw a strange shape skimming through the waves above them. "Wait! I see something!" said the rabbit.

Buster shivered with fright and shrank deeper into Brown-Ears' pocket. "Two of them! We're doomed! It's been nice knowing you."

"Look at that!" cried Brown-Ears. And then, "No, it can't be . . ."

"Don't tell me," squeaked Buster shrilly. "I don't want to know."

"Oh! Look! There's another one! They aren't sharks at all!"

"What then?" moaned the frightened crab. "Killer whales?"

"Mermaids," said Brown-Ears. "I think it's mermaids."

18

Mermaids

Buster peeked out from Brown-Ears' pocket to peer up at the sea surface and saw the long, smooth shapes frolicking in the waves far above them. "See?" said the rabbit. "Mermaids."

Unlikely as it sounds, it did appear to be so. The mermaids rolled and tumbled and dived, spinning round and round each other. Now there were five, and a moment later, three more. And then . . . "Look! A whole *school* of them!"

I don't know if "school" is the right word, but there were a bunch – that is, a good-sized gang of merpeople – all larking about in the water as if they didn't have a care in the world. Of course, merfolk don't, do they? I mean, they don't have to study their mathematics, make their beds, rake the leaves, or pick up their dirty socks. They don't even have to tie their shoes, or wash their hands for supper.

All they have to do is loll about on sandy beaches, take a relaxing swim now and then, and eat tasty things like prawns and clams and oysters. A merperson's life is one big endless happy holiday.

While the two friends sat watching the merfolk and half-wishing that *they* were merpeople, too, one of the smaller mermaids thought it would be fun to go exploring among the rocks below. That's the way merfolk are, you see. Think it looks fun, and away they go. Simply marvellous!

The mermaid swam closer, and Brown-Ears noticed that instead of hands it had flippers; and smooth, sleek fur instead of flowing, long hair. It had small round ears, a black nose, two bright, black button eyes, and bristly whiskers . . .

Wait a minute. Surely mermaids didn't have whiskers?

"That's not a mermaid," Buster confirmed. "It's a seal."

Of course it was. The grey seal pup swam nearer and saw the cloth rabbit sitting on the rock, and streaked towards him. "Wow! Look what I've found!" the pup barked with delight.

"Hello," said Brown-Ears politely. "Pleased to meet you."

"Wow! I've never seen a fish like you before," said the pup. "You don't look like a fish. What kind of fish are you?"

"I'm a toy rabbit, actually. And I was wondering – "

"I'm a seal!" declared the pup proudly. "My name is Toby."

"And a handsome seal you are, Toby," the rabbit told him. "But now that you're here, I was wondering – "

"Seals are best. And grey seals are bestest of all. I'm a *grey* seal. Want to see me swim? I'm a powerful good swimmer, I am. Watch me!"

Instantly, the seal pup began swimming circles round Brown-Ears. He swam backwards, forwards, upside-down and sideways. Looped the loop and spun like a propeller. He twirled and whirled and reeled until Brown-Ears grew dizzy watching him.

"Magnificent," the rabbit called. "Very impressive. I don't know when I've seen such energetic swimming."

Toby smiled happily. "I can go even faster! Want to see?" And he got ready to dart away.

"What I'd really like to see," Brown-Ears said quickly, "is if you could carry something while you swim."

"That's easy! Seals can carry anything. We're powerfully good carriers."

"Could you carry me to the surface, do you think?" wondered the waterlogged rabbit idly.

"Just watch me!" The grey seal swooped him up

between his flippers and sped to the surface like a rocket. Brown-Ears marvelled at the speed of the little seal. In no time at all they were climbing from the waves and on to the rocks where the other seals were playing.

"Hey! Look what I found!" the pup barked, shaking water all around as he scampered up the rocks.

The young grey seals gathered round. "What is it?" they wanted to know. They poked their noses at the bunny and sniffed him up and down; Buster remained well hidden in the front pocket.

"It's a toyrabbit fish," explained Toby. "I found it."

"Where did you find it?" one of the older seals asked.

"Down below. On the rocks where the eels live."

"Ooo, a deep sea creature!" they all exclaimed.

"No, it's not," said the older seal. "Look, it's got fur. It's an air-breather like us."

"What are you going to do with it?" one of the young seals asked. "Keep it?"

"My mum won't let me keep it," sighed Toby glumly. "She never lets me keep anything I find."

"Maybe we can't keep it," said the older seal, "but at least we can have a bit of fun. Follow me!"

With that, he snatched the rabbit in his mouth, and then dived back into the sea before Brown-Ears could say "Hello," or even, "Farewell."

19

The Importance of Not Being Salmon

The seals swam round the rocks and into the bay, yapping and carrying on like a pack of happy hounds. They played a game of Backwards Tag, where the seal with Brown-Ears tried to keep away from the others – leaping, splashing, diving, zig-zagging through the waves and over the rocks. Once the seal carrying the rabbit was tagged by another, he tossed the toy bunny through the air to one of his friends, and the game began all over again.

And when the seals grew tired of this game, they played Fling the Bunny, where one seal would stand on a rock, balancing Brown-Ears on the end of his nose, and then "fling the bunny" into the sea as far as he could. The seal who reached Brown-Ears first was the one to fling him next.

After that, they played the ever-popular Dunk

'n' Tussle, and then a rousing round of Underwater Hurly Burly, followed by a bracing game of No-Hands Hockey. It was all splendid fun – for the seals, that is.

Unfortunately, Brown-Ears found it rather less to his liking. What with all the pitching and tossing, hurling and burling, dunking and tussling, it was a wonder that his poor old floppy head didn't flop right off! His dangerously dangly arm dangled even more dangerously, and his legs were seriously loose. His natty blue bloomers were torn worse than ever, and he feared his stuffing had begun to poke out in places.

Brown-Ears tried to be a good sport. He really did. But when the seals decided to play Tug O' War, he felt things had gone quite far enough. And so had someone else: Toby's mother, who appeared just at that moment. "Nap time everyone!" she barked sharply. "No dilly-dallying – come along."

"Aww, nuts!" complained the young seals. But they did as they were told and began slithering up out of the sea and on to the rocks for their naps – all of them except the older pup, who snatched up Brown-Ears and began swimming very fast in the opposite direction.

He swam to a row of orange fishermen's floats that were bobbing in the water on the other side of the rocks from where the seals were camped.

With a quick upward flip of his back flippers, down he went.

"Oh no!" groaned Buster, "Not back down again!"

Seals are great tricksters. They love nothing more than a joke or a prank. They'll do anything for a laugh. And the older seal had thought of a splendid joke to play on the fishermen. Instead of stealing a fish from the fishermen's nets – which is the one joke seals love more than any other – he would put one back.

Perhaps, on second thoughts, he'd *trade* a fish for a fish. Yes! Better and better!

So down he went, chortling over his amazing sense of humour. The seal came to the net and, taking Brown-Ears' right leg in his mouth, carefully pushed the leg through one of the meshes. Next he took Brown-Ears' right arm and pushed it through another mesh, and then his left leg and arm through two others, and his ears last of all.

"Wait till the fishermen see you!" The seal patted Brown-Ears with a flipper and, stealing a nearby fish from the net, raced off, yelping with laughter at his wonderful trick. What a joke! What a laugh! Oh, this young pup was too clever by half.

"Woe is us," moaned Buster sadly. "So it's come to this: strung up like fish in a net. After all we've been through. We nearly made it."

"Don't you worry, Buster," Brown-Ears told him. "Things are about to go our way."

"We're in a salmon net! Look around you; this net is nearly full," the crab wailed. "I don't know about you, but where I come from it's the end of the line."

"Maybe for a salmon," replied the rabbit. "But we're *not* salmon."

"Salmon, crab – what's the difference? It's the last stop on the way to the Big Aquarium in the Sky," whimpered Buster. "Woe is us."

"Never give up," Brown-Ears told him. "Because you *never* know what's going to happen next."

"You can say *that* again," murmured the crab. But of course the rabbit didn't.

20

So Close, Yet Still So Far Away

Time dragged by. Hour after hour, the two friends hung in the net together. Waiting for whatever would happen next.

"I'm so-o-o depressed," moaned the crab. "We're no better off than before. We should have stayed with the eels!"

"Steady on, Buster," soothed the rabbit. "It's going to be all right. Really it is."

"How can you say that?" wondered Buster. "Look at you – you're floppier than ever! I don't know what's holding you together. If it weren't for all those chains and ribbons round your neck, you would have lost your head long ago!"

That was a fact. Poor old Brown-Ears' wobbly head was hanging by a thread. And a very thin thread at that. Still the brave bunny refused to give up. "It doesn't matter," he told the mournful crab.

"When I get home, McRoss will fix me up as good as new."

"Seeing is believing," sighed Buster.

That's the way with some people. They won't believe anything they can't see. But Brown-Ears knew his master loved him, and that made all the difference. Brown-Ears, true friend and boon companion, knew a thing or two about love. He knew how strong it was, and how stubborn.

A few more hours passed. The sun sank lower and lower towards the sea. Every now and then the little crab would let out a sad sigh, just to let Brown-Ears know he was still very depressed.

"It won't be long now, Buster," the rabbit said. "Have hope."

The words were no sooner out of his mouth than they heard the throaty thrum of a boat engine. The sound grew louder and then stopped. A moment later, they felt a jerk. "Hang on tight!" cried Brown-Ears. "Here we go!"

WHEE! Up went the net! And then . . . PLA-PLOOSH! they were swinging through the bright, shining air.

The net swung up! Down came the fish! A whole boat-load of fish! Two big fishermen in high boots waded in to sort the catch. The good fish were tossed into the hold, the bad fish – like dogfish and lumpfish and pipefish – were tossed back into the sea. The fishermen tossed this way and that, throwing fish right and left. Until they came to a fuzzy brown fish with two long ears.

"Och! What have we here?" said the first fisherman. "Would you look at this now, Gordon!"

"What is it, Angus?" asked the second fisherman.

"It appears to be a rabbit, Gordie."

"A rabbit, Angus? You don't say."

"But I do say it, Gordon. Have a look here yourself."

Fisherman Gordon, holding a mackerel in each hand, stepped up and peered into Brown-Ears' face and smiled. "Bless me, it *is* a rabbit!" he said with a laugh. "However did you get in our net, rascal?"

"I've lived a long time on the sea, Gordie," said the first fisherman. "A long time, I confess. But I've never seen a sea-faring rabbit before this very day."

"Nor have I, Angus. Nor have I."

Angus laughed and propped the cloth rabbit on a box of tackle. "There's a good place for you, my friend. You can begin drying yourself out while we do our work."

Dry! Oh, what a treat! Brown-Ears wanted nothing more than to lie back, close his eyes, and bask in the warm sunshine. He could almost feel his soggy self begin to dry out. It was pure bliss. Well, *almost*.

If you have ever been on a fishing-boat, you will know that they do not sit still for a moment. They bounce. They rock. They toss from side to side in the waves. Brown-Ears, of course, knew nothing of fishing-boats. If he imagined a blissful nap in the sun, he was badly mistaken. A hard ride on a wild horse would have been closer to the mark.

Up! Down! Up! Down! and FLOOP! The soggy bunny slid right off the tackle box and into a crate of fish. OOF! Other fish began plummeting into the crate around him and in a moment he was completely buried in cold, wet mackerel.

"Well, this is a fine kettle of fish, I must say," grumbled Buster. "So much for the great sea rescue. We're worse off than ever! Next stop: the ice house."

"Buck up, Buster," Brown-Ears said in his most encouraging voice. "We can't give up hope now."

"Why not?" moaned the little crab. "Let's give up now and avoid the rush."

It is often said that it's always darkest just before the dawn. If that is true, then this was surely that darkest hour, because Brown-Ears did not see how it could possibly get any darker. But then, he did not know what went on in an ice house. He would soon find out.

21
A Wanted Rabbit

The little fishing-boat entered the harbour and chugged to the wharf. The crates of fish were unloaded and hurried off to the ice house where the fish would be sorted. The best fish would be packed in boxes of ice and shipped off to fish markets in London and Paris. And the rest? Well, where do you think fish fingers come from?

The crate holding Brown-Ears and Buster was carried into the ice house with all the rest. Then, one by one, the fishermen and their helpers began sorting the fish and packing them away in boxes of ice. When the last box was packed, they put on their rubber aprons and reached for their sharp knives. Then they reached into the crates for the fish.

"It's been nice knowing you, Brown-Ears," whispered Buster.

Before Brown-Ears could reply he felt a hand

seize him round the middle and he was yanked up and out of the crate. An instant later, he found himself looking into the wide blue eyes of a startled red-headed boy. "Hey!" the boy shouted. "What's this?"

One of the fishermen spied the bunny and called out, "Ho there, Angus! There's yer wee friend."

The fisherman named Angus stepped over to the boy. "I wondered where the rascal had got to." He pointed to the toy rabbit. "Here you are, Jackie lad, meet Mr Sea Hare."

"Wherever did you get that?" asked one of the other helpers. "It's sopping wet."

"Oh, aye – he's sopping wet," said Angus. "I fished him from the sea. Where else would I get a sea hare?"

The others laughed. "Caught him in your net did you, Angus?"

"Hoot, man! Is that not what I'm telling you?"

"What are you going to do with him?" asked the helper.

"Well," said Angus, scratching his head. "I dinna know what to do with him. You take him, Jackie, my boy. He's all yours."

"A little old to be carrying a cuddly toy aren't you, Jackie-boy?" The fishermen laughed and went back to their work.

Jackie blushed and made to toss the soggy toy

into the rubbish bin. But something about the bunny caught his eye and he stopped. He looked at the toy rabbit more closely. He saw the tattered blue bloomers and the dangly limbs and dangerously floppy head. Then he saw the thing that had caught his eye: the small collection of coloured ribbons and beaded chains wrapped so carefully round the bunny's neck.

It was clear to Jackie that someone loved this toy rabbit very much. He remembered a time – not all that long ago, really – when he himself had a soft toy that he carried with him everywhere.

And he remembered something else: a poster on the jetty.

"Let's see what we can do for you," Jackie said. He turned and placed Brown-Ears on the stone table before him. Then, very carefully, he began to clean up the bunny with fresh water. He washed off the slime and the fishy smell, wrapped Brown-Ears in a towel and put him on a shelf near the window. "Wait there," the boy told him. "I'll fetch you when I'm finished."

22

Catch of the Day

McRoss and his mum were just sitting down to a bit of tea when there came a knock on the door. McRoss's mother answered the door and saw a young stranger, dressed in fisherman's clothes, standing on the step with a white bundle under his arm.

"Good afternoon," the boy said pleasantly. "May I interest you in the catch of the day?" The red-haired young fisherman held out the bundle, which was wrapped in white butcher's paper.

"Well, I don't know – " McRoss's mum said. "We were having tea just now. Perhaps another time."

"Certainly," said the boy, with a twinkle in his eye. "But it's a prize catch, it is. I think you'll find it worth your while."

"We don't eat much fish," said Mum. "Thank you all the same. Goodbye." She started to close the door.

But the young fisherman was persistent. He leaned forward. "Well, perhaps your son would like to take a wee look at least."

"Could I, Mum?" asked McRoss. He had seen the white bundle and was curious. No fisherman had ever come to the door before. It must be a fine fish, this catch of the day. "Please, Mum. Could I?"

"But your tea is getting cold, dear."

"Won't take a moment," said the fisherman. "May I?" He stepped in through the door.

"Yes, come in. But only for a moment, mind."

The older boy handed the package to McRoss, who promptly sat down cross-legged on the floor and began untying it. The white paper fell away.

And all of a sudden there he was, in the flesh – in the fuzz, that is – his old, floppy, happy-go-lucky, friend-to-all brown self . . .

"Brown-Ears!" cried McRoss, snatching up the still-soggy rabbit and hugging him tight. "He's back! Look everyone! Brown-Ears is back! I knew he would come home again! I knew it!"

McRoss's mum sank to her knees beside her little boy. "I don't believe it," she said, shaking her head again and again. She reached out a hand to touch the bunny. "Oh! But he's soaking wet!"

"So would you be," said Jackie, "if you'd been hauled fresh from the sea. I told you he was the catch of the day, and so he is!" He bent down beside McRoss. "Now then, laddie, is this the wayward beastie?"

"It is! Yes, it is!" cried McRoss happily, clasping the dripping bunny to him. "Thank you! Thank you, for bringing my good friend back to me."

"That's all right," said Jackie, beaming with pleasure. "I know how it is when you've got a special friend. I used to have one, too. Binker the Bear – that was mine."

"I still don't believe it," said McRoss's mum again. "I thought we'd seen the last of him. But McRoss was sure he'd come home; he never gave up hope. However did you know where to bring Brown-Ears?"

The fisherboy reached into his pocket and brought out a folded piece of paper. He unfolded it and read: "Wanted: Wet or Dry – Brown-Ears. Reward. If found please ring R. Dundee." He held up the paper and pointed to the address written on the bottom.

"It's one of my posters," remarked McRoss. "Remember, Mum?"

"You see? I had specific directions," Jackie said, and stepped to the door. "I'll be saying good night to you now." He walked to the front gate, turned and waved goodbye.

"Thank you," called McRoss's mother. "And God bless you!"

"Wait a minute!" McRoss shouted, and ran to

the gate. "What about the reward I promised?"

The fisherlad turned round with a big, happy grin. "Don't give it another thought," Jackie said. "I've already had my reward! Cheerio!"

23

A Bit of a Miracle

Home at last! Brown-Ears was so happy he thought he'd burst. And McRoss was so happy he could hardly stand still – he kept jumping up and down and clutching his cuddly toy to him, saying, "I knew you'd come back, Brown-Ears! I knew it!"

McRoss's mum laughed out loud to see her little boy so happy. She reached out a hand to pat the bunny, and felt something move under her hand. "What's this? Why, I do believe there's a wee friend in his pocket!"

McRoss peeked into Brown-Ears' pocket and saw Buster. "It's a hermit crab!" he declared. "Can I keep it?"

"Well, I don't know," his mother said doubtfully – which is what grown-ups always say whenever you ask them if you can keep some special thing you've found – "you'll have to find him a place to live. He'll need looking after."

McRoss ran off to find Buster a new home, and McRoss's mum looked at the limp and soggy rabbit: his dangly arms and legs, and the head hanging dangerously by a single frayed thread. The cuddly brown fur was matted and salt-crusted; stuffing was showing through in places; the spiffy blue bloomers were tattered and torn; and he squelched when squeezed. "Tch-tch! Such a state!" she sighed. "Whatever have you been up to, Mr Brown-Ears?"

McRoss returned with a glass jar for Buster and found his mother examining his scruffy friend. "He'll be all right . . . won't he, Mum?" McRoss asked worriedly.

His mother bit her lip. "I can't promise he'll be good as new, but we'll try." She picked up the rabbit and examined him closely, poking him here and there. "Right! We've got work to do!"

Work they did. First they undressed the bunny, wrapped him in a towel, and began kneading him gently. When they had pressed out as much sea water as they could, they filled a big basin with hot water and shampooed him with laundry soap. Then they wrapped him in a dry towel and wrung him out. It took three basins of clean water and four dry towels to squeeze out the last of the salt.

Brown-Ears enjoyed the warm bath, and adored all the hugs and squeezes. Then McRoss fetched his mum's sewing-basket and she sat down with scissors, needle and thread to set things right. The dangly arm was snipped free – which worried the cloth rabbit somewhat – then the other arm and the threads of both loose legs were cut as well.

"Sorry, Brown-Ears," McRoss's mum soothed, "but it's got to be done."

She worked quickly, threading the needle and sewing the loose limbs back on, nice and tight. When she had finished, the fuzzy toy's arms and legs were solidly attached once more.

"Now for the tricky bit," she said, and began unwrapping the ribbons and beaded chains from around the rabbit's neck. "You know," she said, as her fingers untied the ribbons, "I think these bits of ribbon held your friend together."

"Really?" wondered McRoss.

"I'm certain of it. Wherever did they come from?"

"I put them there," said McRoss.

"Why?" asked Mum.

"Because I love him," the little boy answered. "I wanted him to look nice."

"Well, that's what kept him together. Without them, he would have fallen apart long ago."

Sure enough, when the last brass chain had been unclasped and the last bit of coloured ribbon untied, that last frazzled thread gave way. "Not to worry," McRoss's mum said, "I'll soon have that repaired." Her quick fingers sewed the head back

on to the shoulders in no time flat. When she had finished, all the various parts were firmly attached once more, and Brown-Ears felt better than ever.

At last, Mum picked up the blue bloomers. "These are a loss, I'm afraid," she said. "But they'll serve as a pattern for some new ones. We will go to the shops tomorrow and buy some material." She turned to her son and cupped his chin in her hand. "But now, my love, it's bedtime for all of us."

Later that night, when the house was dark and quiet, McRoss's mum tiptoed to her little boy's room. Brown-Ears lay wrapped in a towel, snuggled beside his master. Buster, wearing his new whelk shell, was curled up fast asleep in a glass jar next to the bed. She stood for a moment, looking down at the three of them, all sleeping so peacefully. Then she bent and kissed her son goodnight. She also patted Brown-Ears, and told him, "I thought you were lost for good, but McRoss never doubted you would come back. It's a bit of a miracle, really."

She stood up to leave, and her eye fell upon the neatly tied ribbons little McRoss had placed once more round his good friend Brown-Ears' neck. "Held together with love," she whispered softly. "So are we all."